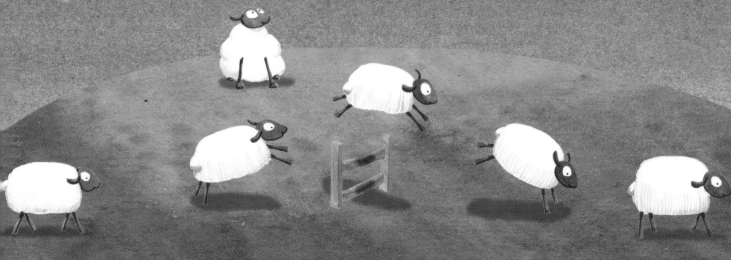

Little Cloud Lamb

LIGHT Series

© 2010 CUENTO DE LUZ SL
Calle Claveles 10, Urb. Monteclaro
Pozuelo de Alarcon, 28223 Madrid, Spain

www.cuentodeluz.com

Text © Ana A. de Eulate
Illustrations © Monica Carretero
English translation by Jon Brokenbrow

ISBN: 978-84-938240-2-0
DL: M-47440-2010

Printed by Graficas AGA in Madrid, Spain,
November 2010, print number 65691

FSC
www.fsc.org

MIX
Paper from
responsible sources
FSC® C003935

Ana A. de Eulate

Little Cloud Lamb

Illustrations by Monica Carretero

CUENTO
DE LUZ

One night, under the light of the full moon and the stars, a lamb was born.

Molly, his mother, lay next to him in the meadow, tired but happy as she gazed lovingly at her new baby.

"Lambkin, now that's a fine name," she thought as she licked his four little legs and rosy body.

The following morning, as soon as the sun came up, the other sheep in the flock trotted over to congratulate Molly.

A few weeks after he was born, Molly began to notice that instead of having wool growing on his body, Lambkin looked different, and was covered with a small, fluffy, white cloud.

A real cloud that had fallen from the sky and come to rest on her son's four legs.

A cloudy cloud, with storms, lightning and sudden rain, but also with the sun shining through.

Lambkin got bigger and bigger, but because he had a cloud instead of a woolly coat, he grew apart from the other lambs, who found him different and didn't know how to play with him.

And so he spent many hours sitting on his own, gazing out towards the horizon and watching the plants and animals. He soon found a way of talking that he enjoyed.

He would have long, silent conversations with the snails; he would watch the grass growing, and how the flowers opened. Something inside him grew and grew, making him stronger, as if the sun's rays had shone through his cloudy body.

Some nights, the other sheep in the flock would disappear for a few hours.

They left to jump over the fences that appeared like invisible drawings in the minds of people who couldn't get to sleep, and who counted the sheep over and over again.

Lambkin, who usually woke up at daybreak, often saw them walking back slowly to the meadow, exhausted from so much jumping and complaining about their sore hooves.

"When I'm grown up, I don't want to jump over fences for people who can't get to sleep," he thought.

"I'll help them to do it, but another way..."

Lambkin was very sensitive. In his world, musical notes flew through the air together with the butterflies. He played in a different way because he felt it was more creative, and more artistic.

Sometimes he felt sad to see how the other lambs would fight, cheat each other or tell lies.

Whenever this happened, Lambkin would cry so much that the next day, the place where his tears had fallen would be covered in poppies.

One afternoon, the little lamb became ill, and the nights went by with all their hours, and the months with all their days, but he didn't get better. Molly stayed at his side, keeping his shivering body warm.

And then, one spring morning, Lambkin fell asleep forever. When she realized he would not wake up, Molly looked down at him lovingly, and was suddenly surprised to see that the cloud that had once been his body was no longer there. It had evaporated!

In its place there was wool. Yes, the same wool that all the other lambs wore, but much, much whiter, and gleaming with light.

And then, Molly looked up into the sky, dried her tears, and there she saw it.

It was the brightest, most beautiful cloud of all; it was Lambkin's cloud.

At night, when children cannot get to sleep, a white cloud, the softest, brightest cloud of them all, comes to visit them.

It comes to rest on their eyes like cotton wool, slowly closing them. And then the cloud leads them to the land of dreams, where they wake up amongst rainbows and musical notes.

In that magical waking moment, when you look carefully with the eyes we all have inside us, you will see how a little lamb appears, with a happy, smiling face.

The little lamb whose body was a cloud.

Cuento de Luz (Tale of Light) publishes stories that enlighten our lives to bring out our inner child. Stories that make time stand still for us to live the present. Stories that take the imagination on a journey and help care for our planet, to respect differences, break down barriers and promote peace. Stories that do not leave you indifferent; stories that lift you up.

Cuento de Luz respects the environment and contributes to the protection of nature, incorporating sustainability principles through eco-friendly publishing.

CUENTO
DE LUZ